Green Queen

by Marci Peschke
illustrated by Tuesday Mourning

PICTURE WINDOW BOOKS
a capstone imprint

Kylie Jean is published by Picture Window Books
A Capstone Imprint
1710 Roe Crest Drive
North Mankato, Minnesota 56003
www.capstoneyoungreaders.com

Library of Congress Cataloging-in-Publication Data
Peschke, M. (Marci), author.
Green queen / by Marci Peschke ; illustrated by Tuesday Mourning.
pages cm. -- (Kylie Jean)
ISBN 978-1-4795-2351-1 (hardcover) -- ISBN 978-1-4795-3813-3 (paper over board)
1. Earth Day--Texas--Juvenile fiction. 2. Playgrounds--Texas--Juvenile fiction. 3. Cities and towns--Texas--Juvenile fiction. 4. Elementary schools--Texas--Juvenile fiction. 5. Texas--Juvenile fiction. [1. Earth Day--Fiction. 2. Playgrounds--Fiction. 3. City and town life--Fiction. 4. Schools--Fiction. 5. Texas--Fiction.] I. Mourning, Tuesday, illustrator. II. Title. III. Series: Peschke, M. (Marci) Kylie Jean.
PZ7.P441245Gr 2014
813.6--dc23

2013028543

Summary: Earth Day is coming, and Kylie Jean and the other second graders decide that the perfect way to celebrate is to clean up and beautify the school playground — and the whole town.

Graphic Designer: Kristi Carlson

Editor: Alison Deering

Production Specialist: Eric Manske

Design Element Credit:
Shutterstock/blue67design

Printed in China.
092013
007738LEOS14

For the REAL true Granny,
with love for Rick
—MP

Table of Contents

All About Me, Kylie Jean! 7

Chapter 1
Recycling Roundup 11

Chapter 2
Green Makeover 14

Chapter 3
Playground Pride 24

Chapter 4
Playground Project 29

Chapter 5
Neat News 34

Chapter 6
More Trees, Please 42

Chapter 7
Going Green 48

Chapter 8
Gardens Galore 55

Chapter 9
VIPs 66

Chapter 10
Parade Preparations 76

Chapter 11
Garden Club Queen 86

Chapter 12
Earth Day 97

TJ

All About Me, Kylie Jean!

My name is Kylie Jean Carter. I live in a big, sunny, yellow house on Peachtree Lane in Jacksonville, Texas with Momma, Daddy, and my two brothers, T.J. and Ugly Brother.

T.J. is my older brother, and Ugly Brother is . . . well . . . he's really a dog. Don't you go telling him he is a dog. Okay? I mean it. He thinks he is a real true person.

He is a black-and-white bulldog. His front looks like his back, all smashed in. His face is all droopy like he's sad, but he's not.

His two front teeth stick out, and his tongue hangs down. (Now you know why his name is Ugly Brother.)

Everyone I love to the moon and back lives in Jacksonville. Nanny, Pa, Granny, Pappy, my aunts, my uncles, and my cousins all live here. I'm extra lucky, because I can see all of them any time I want to!

My momma says I'm pretty. She says I have eyes as blue as the summer sky and a smile as sweet as an angel. (Momma says pretty is as pretty does. That means being nice to the old folks, taking care of little animals, and respecting my momma and daddy.)

But I'm pretty on the outside and on the inside. My hair is long, brown, and curly.

I wear it in a ponytail sometimes, but my absolute most favorite is when Momma pulls it back in a princess style on special days.

I just gave you a little hint about my big dream. Ever since I was a bitty baby I have wanted to be an honest-to-goodness beauty queen. I even know the wave. It's side to side, nice and slow, with a dazzling smile. I practice all the time, because everybody knows beauty queens need to have a perfect wave.

I'm Kylie Jean, and I'm going to be a beauty queen. Just you wait and see!

Chapter 1
Recycling Roundup

When I walk outside, I can tell right away that spring is in the air! The bees are a-buzzin' and hummingbirds are a-hummin'. The leaves on the dogwood trees are covered with delicate white blooms, like blossoms on a bride's gown.

Every few feet I see a redbud tree showered with pixie-sized purple flowers. Wildflowers of every kind and color tumble over the greenest grass you've ever seen.

A warm breeze sails through the windows on the school bus, and I smile. It's spring, all right! And that means that Earth Day is almost here!

Every year, our town holds a big parade to celebrate Earth Day. Jacksonville loves a parade. A few of our favorite parades are Homecoming, Santa's Sleigh, Rodeo, Blueberry Festival, Thanksgiving Day, Veteran's Day, and the Fourth of July, so you see what I mean.

Just thinking about the Earth Day parade makes me so happy I could sing a sweet song like a white-winged dove.

I'm quiet for a change as I look at all the spring flowers outside. That's when I hear some fifth graders in front of me talking about their student council project.

"A recycling roundup is perfect," a tall girl says. "We can put recycling cans around school. Some will be for paper, some will be for aluminum cans, and some will be for plastic and glass."

"That's the perfect plan!" the girl beside her agrees. "Especially because it's almost Earth Day!"

Hearing about their project makes me want to do something, too, but those big kids never think second graders can do anything.

As I listen, an idea suddenly hits my brain like dew drops on green grass. I will come up with my own way to celebrate Earth Day!

Chapter 2
Green Makeover

The next day at school, I can't wait to talk to my friends about Earth Day. It's less than two weeks away! As soon as I walk into my classroom, I spot Cara, Lucy, and Paula.

"Hey, y'all," I say. "The big kids are doing a recycling project for Earth Day. I need you to help me think up the perfect second-grade project."

My friends are all quiet for a long time. I watch the hands on the clock move slowly. I hope they think of something soon, or the bell will ring!

I wait and wait. Paula scribbles some notes on her paper. I wait some more.

Cara suddenly gasps. "I've got it!" she shouts, dragging us over to the window by the playground. "What do you see out there?"

Outside some boys are running around the playground. They jump on the sit-n-spin and run under the slide. If they don't get to class soon, they'll be late!

Lucy shrugs. "A playground," she says. "What am I supposed to see?"

I press my face against the window glass, hoping to see what Cara is seeing. But I don't even know what I'm supposed to be looking for.

"Our playground is really dirty!" Cara says.

Cara is right. There are pieces of trash lying on the ground and dead leaves hugging the edge of the fence. On the far side of the playground, one swing is missing part of its chain. It dangles in the wind like an odd bird with a broken wing. And the flower beds are full of dirt, just begging for some spring flowers.

"We can clean it up for Earth Day!" Cara says.

Lucy, Paula, and I nod. "Cleaning up the playground is going to be a lot of work," Lucy says. "It could take weeks to get everything done!"

"We need some more kids to help us!" I say.

"I think we need a grown-up to help us, too," Paula says. "We should go talk to Ms. Corazón."

"That's a great idea!" I say. Paula is so smart.

We don't waste a single minute. Our teacher is writing today's assignments on the board, so I march right up and tap her on the arm.

"Yes, Kylie Jean?" she replies as she keeps on writing. She doesn't even look, but she knows it's me! Maybe that saying about teachers having eyes in the backs of their heads is true!

"Can we talk to you?" I ask.

Ms. Corazón turns around and looks at us. "Is everything okay?" she asks.

"We're fine," Lucy says. "But everything is not okay. Our playground is sad and dirty!"

I add, "We want to give it a makeover for Earth Day!"

Ms. Corazón walks over to the window. "I see what you mean," she says with a frown. "Maybe the other second grade class can help us?"

I exclaim, "Oh, what a great idea!"

"I told you we needed a grown-up!" Paula says.

Ms. Corazón sits down at her desk and writes a note. "Will you girls take this down to the principal's office?" she asks.

Lucy, Paula, Cara, and I nod. We're super curious about what the note says, but we don't peek. We hand it to the school secretary, who reads the note, makes a quick phone call, and writes out another note for us to take back to our teacher.

"The principal will meet us on the playground during recess!" Ms. Corazón says when she finishes reading the note.

"Yay!" we all cheer. Our playground project is taking off!

Ms. Corazón decides to let us work on our playground plan instead of doing our science assignment. My friends and I sit down to brainstorm ideas. We are studying the environment, so we promise to reuse, recycle, and renew items on the playground.

“We can repair and repaint the old equipment!” Cara says.

“And reuse the old wooden trash barrels to make new planters!” Lucy adds.

“Maybe we could get someone to donate some old grain barrels,” I suggest. “We can recycle them into trash cans!”

While Cara and I write out the plan, Lucy and Paula work on drawing what we have in mind. Lucy suggests we get some extra barrels for recycling soda cans and water bottles as well. We also want to put new plants in the flower beds and planters.

“Don’t forget to add stepping stones for a walking path,” Cara reminds me.

I nod. "How about some benches to sit on, too?" I suggest.

"I love that idea!" Lucy agrees. "Paula and I will draw them by the flower beds."

Right before recess, we show Ms. Corazón our work. "You girls have done a great job!" she tells us. "I'm sure Mr. Johnson will support our playground project when he sees this!"

We line up and head outside. The principal, Mr. Johnson, is waiting for us by the broken swings. He is wearing a brown suit and a tie with little green leaves on it. "Hello, girls," he says. "I hear you have an idea to spruce up our playground. Do you have your plans written down?"

Cara hands him a green folder. "Yes, sir, we do," she replies politely.

trash

Mr. Johnson studies our plan and drawings. "Girls, I am impressed," he says. "You saw a problem and came up with a plan to fix it."

My friends and I grin at each other. We are happy as can be about our playground project!

"Do you have a timeline for getting this done?" Mr. Johnson asks us.

I nod eagerly. "Yes, sir. The sooner, the better!"

My friends and I decide Saturday will be our playground-makeover day. That will give us a few days to get ready and get supplies for our project.

My friends and I call ourselves the Green Team! We are so excited. The best part is, when we're done, our playground will be a safe place for kids to play, and it will be good for planet Earth, too!

Chapter 3
Playground Pride

When I tell my family about my playground plans after school that day, they are so proud of me. "What a great idea, sugar," Momma says.

"Where are you going to get the flowers and plants?" Daddy asks me.

"I'm going to ask for donations," I say. "That way, everyone can help celebrate Earth Day!"

I decide to ask Miss Clarabelle, my next-door neighbor, to help. She works at Hillside Nursery.

“I’m sure we can make a donation,” Miss Clarabelle says. She calls the nursery, and they agree to give us some beautiful flowers.

Next I call Granny. She’s a member of the Garden Club and has a real green thumb.

“Of course I’ll help you, Kylie Jean,” Granny tells me. “And I’m sure the rest of the Garden Club ladies would be happy to help plant flowers. I’ll ask them at our next meeting.”

I smile. My Earth Day project is in full bloom!

* * *

When Lucy and I get on the bus on the next morning, I sit in my favorite spot, right behind Mr. Jim, our bus driver. Lucy sits down next to me.

“Mr. Jim, I need a favor,” I tell him.

"What do you need me to do?" Mr. Jim asks.

I smile sweetly. "You're pretty handy with tools," I say. "Remember that day the bus broke down and you fixed it? Well, I have some playground equipment that needs to be fixed, and I think you'd be perfect for the job!"

Mr. Jim scratches his bearded chin. "I reckon I can do that for you kids," he replies.

"Fantastic!" I exclaim. "We are having a work day on the playground on Saturday, so please plan to come and don't forget to bring your tools."

Lucy gives me a high five. Then she shares some big news. "I called my uncle last night. When I told him about our playground plan, he offered to donate some old grain barrels from his farm for our trash and recycling containers!"

I think that good news deserves another high five!

Later at school, we just keep getting more good news. Paula and Cara were able to get some donations and sign up volunteers, too!

"I told everyone at church last night about our plan," Paula says. "The youth group volunteered to paint all of the old equipment! Now we just need to get the paint donated and choose a color."

"We already have paint!" Cara says. "My daddy and I went to the hardware store. The owner offered to donate paint that doesn't smell bad. It's better for people, animals, and the earth."

"I bet I know what color you want, Kylie Jean!" Lucy says.

Everyone knows my favorite color is pink. "Pink is my best color, but it might not be right for a playground," I tell her.

"I think we should paint everything green," Paula says. "It's a nature color. Plus, it'll blend in so we can enjoy the pretty plants and flowers."

"Paula, you are a paint-picking genius!" I tell her, and everyone else agrees.

Chapter 4
Playground Project

I wake up bright and early on Saturday morning and put on my pink gardening boots and work clothes. Momma, Daddy, T.J., Ugly Brother, and I all pile into Momma's van.

When we pull into the school parking lot, it's packed. We hear banging, clanging, and scraping. Mr. Jim and the church youth group are hard at work. Paula and her parents are painting.

Everywhere we look, second graders are helping. It's hard to find my best cousin Lucy, but finally I spot her standing with Cara.

"I thought you'd never get here!" Lucy says when I walk over. "We're picking up trash. Can you help us?"

I pull my pink work gloves out of my pocket. "I sure can!" I reply. "And I brought a helper, too."

I turn to Ugly Brother and ask, "Ugly Brother, do you want to help us?"

He barks, "Ruff, ruff." That means yes. Then he fetches an old juice box for me to put in the trash.

The principal sees us and waves. He is helping Ms. Corazón put down some stepping stones so the grass won't get trampled.

Daddy and T.J. are hard at work cutting the old wooden trash barrels to make the new planters. The church kids are covering everything with paint the color of green leaves. Mr. Jim is testing the swing — it looks as good as new!

Across the playground, I see Momma helping Miss Clarabelle, Granny, and the Garden Club ladies. They are planting pretty new flowers in the old flower beds.

Just then I notice some broken daisies in the bottom of a box, and an idea hits my brain like a caterpillar on a juicy leaf. I can recycle them into a crown!

Some of the stems are short and some are long, but I weave those daisies together in no time. Then I carefully put on my crown.

Lucy giggles when she sees me. "You look like Mother Nature!" she says.

Cara says, "I bet she's trying to be the playground queen."

I laugh. Being the playground queen does sound fun. "Just call me the Green Queen!" I tell my friends.

Lucy says, "Okay, Green Queen, let's help finish this project."

We work and work. The playground is looking better and better!

Finally, Mr. Johnson calls everyone over to the playground gate. "I want to thank everyone for helping us make our playground such a great place for kids to play," he says.

Everyone claps and cheers.

"Many of you know this project was possible because of the vision and hard work of our second-grade students, especially Cara, Kylie Jean, Paula, and Lucy," Mr. Johnson says. "Let's hear it for the Green Team!"

Everyone cheers even louder! Our playground looks awesome with the new path, cheerful flowers, and freshly painted equipment. The work is done, and we're ready to play!

Chapter 5
Neat News

Later that night, I am sitting in the living room working on my homework. Our assignment is to make something from recycled trash. I am using old magazines to make a necklace. I cut the pages into strips, dip them in water and a little glue, and roll each strip into a bead.

Just then, the news comes on, and I see something that makes me shout with excitement! "Momma, Daddy, T.J., come quick," I holler. "Granny is on the news!"

Ugly Brother barks and barks, and I have to make him hush because I can't hear. Momma, Daddy, and T.J. come running just in time to hear Granny explain that our town, Jacksonville, has entered the state of Texas's "Prettiest Town" contest.

"It won't be enough to just pick up some trash," Granny says. "This award is not just about having a pretty town. After all, pretty is as pretty does. We need to do more to show that our community cares about green living, especially since Earth Day is only a week away."

"Wouldn't it be great if Jacksonville won?" Momma says.

I nod. "Then everyone would know how pretty our town is!" I say.

On the news, Granny is still talking. "We will be hosting a tree-planting event tomorrow morning. And The Garden Club will be planting gardens during the next week to help Jacksonville claim the grand prize!" she says.

"Winning this contest might finally make Momma's dream of becoming Garden Club president come true," Daddy says.

"What do you mean?" I ask.

"Granny runs for president of the Garden Club every year," Momma says. "But every year someone else is chosen."

That decides it. "Then Ugly Brother and I need to help Granny win," I say. "I bet we can think of lots of green-living challenges if we put our minds to it!"

“What did you have in mind?” Momma asks.

“How about having people walk or ride their bikes instead of driving their cars?” I suggest.

“Maybe we could talk to the mayor about creating a watering schedule for the town,” Daddy adds. “That would help conserve water.”

“Now that’s a real good idea!” Momma exclaims. “We’ll make Jacksonville as shiny as a pretty new penny.”

Momma calls Granny to tell her about all of our great green ideas. I decide to take a shower instead of a bath because it uses less water. And I turn off the water while I brush my teeth and turn it back on when I am ready to rinse out the toothpaste.

Ugly Brother is waiting for me in my room when I go in. I climb into bed. I need to be well rested to help plant trees in the morning!

Daddy comes to kiss us goodnight. “I love you to the moon and back,” he says, giving me a big squeezy hug.

I squeeze him back and say, “I love you a bushel and a peck and a hug around the neck!”

Daddy turns off the light. I close my eyes and get ready to count some sheep until I fall asleep. Suddenly Ugly Brother jumps right out of bed and starts barking.

“What’s wrong?” I ask. “Are you scared?”

“Ruff!” he barks. That means no. Then he barks some more and sits down.

"Come to bed, you silly doggie." I tell him.

"Ruff!" he barks again.

I look down and see that he is sitting right beside my pink princess night-light. He looks at it, then looks back at me.

"Are you trying to tell me to unplug that light and save energy?" I ask.

"Ruff, ruff!" Ugly Brother barks.

"You're right, Ugly Brother," I agree. "I am a big girl, and second graders do not need night-lights."

After I unplug that night-light, my room is as dark as the inside of a pocket. I see stars twinkling outside, so I make a very special wish.

I bet you think I wished that I was a beauty queen, huh? But if that's what you thought, you'd lose that bet. I wished for Granny to be the next Garden Club president. Then I pull up my covers and decide to count stars instead of sheep.

Chapter 6
More Trees, Please

The next morning, Momma wakes us up bright and early to go help. "Kylie Jean, T.J., Ugly Brother! Wake up!" she calls. "We have to get going. It's time to plant some trees."

T.J. stumbles downstairs looking half-asleep. I think he stayed up all night playing video games again. "I wish I could stay at home and dream about planting trees instead," he says.

Momma puts her hands on her hips, which is never a good sign. T.J. is fixin' to get in trouble!

"Timothy James Carter," Momma says, "you will not sleep through planting the trees. You are a good, strong worker, and Granny needs you today. She needs all of us."

T.J. looks like he feels bad. "I'm sorry, Momma," he says.

Daddy walks into the kitchen just then. "Come on, son," he says to T.J. "You'll wake up on the way over there. We're going to be the best tree-planting team ever."

When we walk outside, Daddy has our bikes waiting in the driveway. As part of our green-living plan, he has been leaving his truck at home and riding his bike to work.

T.J. looks at Momma's van, and I can tell he wants to drive over to the tree planting. But he doesn't say a thing. Instead, he shoves the rest of his toast in his mouth and hops on his bike.

I put on my pink helmet and pedal my pink bike right down Peachtree Lane toward downtown. Ugly Brother can't ride a bike on account of he's a dog, so he runs along beside me.

Before long, we can see the tops of the trees waving at the sky! They are extra tall, waiting in truck beds for us to come and plant them.

In the town square, people in Green Team T-shirts are rushing around like ants at a picnic. Daddy asked his boss at the newspaper to sponsor a T-shirt sale. All the money will go to the Garden Club so they can plant gardens all around town.

Before we get started planting, the mayor welcomes everyone with some exciting news. "The judges have looked at Mrs. Carter's photos and contest application, and Jacksonville is a finalist for the Prettiest Town contest!" he tells the crowd. "Now we really need to get busy planting those trees before the judges come to town."

Granny looks as happy as a bee in a blossom. Everyone comes over to congratulate her.

I give Granny a big squeezy hug. "I'm so proud of you," I tell her.

Granny squeezes me back. "We haven't won yet, little lady, but thank you," she says.

Daddy and T.J. start unloading and planting the trees. Ugly Brother wants to help too. He's a good digger, but you need a big hole for a tree.

"Just let him dig until he gets tired," Daddy says. "He'll quit."

"But Carters aren't quitters," I tell him. "He might just keep on digging till he's all worn out!"

"I'll keep an eye on him, Little Bit," T.J. promises.

With the boys busy, Momma and I get to work passing out cold water to the other people planting.

"Did you know trees keep the soil strong?" I ask them. "It's true. The roots just hug up all that rich, dark dirt and keep it together."

"That's just one good thing about trees," Momma agrees. "They also help clean our air and make shade."

Momma and I look around the town square at all the lovely leafy green trees. I sure do hope they help us win!

After we pass out the last bottle of water, we head over to buy our own T-shirts.

"There are so many people in green T-shirts!" I point out excitedly. "Granny better get ready to plant a lot of flowers."

"If Granny can get the mayor to plant all of these trees, the flowers will be easy," Momma says. "Just you wait and see!"

Chapter 7
Going Green

This year, Jacksonville's Earth Day parade is going to be bigger and better than ever! Daddy's newspaper is going to have a float in the parade, and the Garden Club will have one, too.

Now that our town is a finalist in the Prettiest Town contest, everyone is working extra hard to prove that Jacksonville is pretty inside and out.

During the week, Daddy's newspaper is running stories about green living. They're also passing out tips on how to be kind to the environment.

I already know some of the tips, like taking a shower instead of a bath and turning off the water when you brush your teeth.

Mayor Jenkins liked Daddy's idea and set up a watering schedule, which was printed in the paper. The whole town is divided into zones. Our house is in zone five, which means we can water the grass on Tuesdays, Thursdays, and Sundays.

On Monday evening, I see that Miss Clarabelle is watering her grass. I go right over to see if she knows about the new watering schedule.

When I knock on her door, she comes right away. "Kylie Jean!" she says. "How are you?"

"I'm just fine, thank you for asking," I reply. "But did you know you're in watering zone five now?"

Miss Clarabelle looks confused. “What is watering zone five?” she asks me.

I explain all about Daddy’s plan to save water. Then I show her the story in the paper that has the list of zones and days for watering.

“I guess I missed that page when I was reading the paper,” she tells me. “I’m so glad you came by to tell me.”

Before I go, I remind her, “Don’t forget that your watering days are now Tuesday, Thursday, and Sunday. Okay?”

Miss Clarabelle nods. “I’m going to write it on my calendar,” she says. “Thank you for being a good little neighbor and coming right over to explain it to me.”

As I cross our yard on my way back home, I see my bike has a tire as flat as a fat snake's belly. Oh, no! I run inside to get help.

"T.J., Ugly Brother, come quick!" I holler. "I need help!"

T.J. comes running outside right away. Ugly Brother is right on his heels. "What's wrong?" T.J. asks.

"My bike has a flat tire," I tell him. "I need it to ride to school.

T.J. and Ugly Brother both follow me out to the yard. T.J. looks at the tire. It is flatter than a pancake.

"Let's try to fill it with air first," T.J. suggests. "We need an air pump."

I run into the garage and dig to find Daddy's air pump. It has to be there somewhere! Ugly Brother sees it in the corner and starts barking. He's a real good finder.

T.J. sets up the pump and starts to attach it to the tire when Ugly Brother comes over and tries to sit on it. T.J. laughs. "Hey, Brother, it's not time to pump yet," he says. "Besides, I think you are too short for the job."

T.J. starts to fill the tire. "If the air leaks back out, you'll probably need a new tire," he says. Pump, pump, pump. My tire gets fatter and fuller as the air goes in.

I'm holding my breath, and I have my fingers crossed for luck. "You can help me by crossing your paws for luck. Okay?" I tell Ugly Brother.

"Ruff, ruff!" Ugly Brother barks. He crosses his paws and keeps them crossed.

T.J. finishes pumping, and we watch and wait. The air stays in. Yay!

"Thanks, T.J.!" I say. "Thanks, Ugly Brother!"

It's good to have brothers to help you. Sometimes I wish I had a sister, but I have my best cousin Lucy, so it's okay.

Besides, Momma says when you have sisters, you have to share everything. Looking at my pink bike, I know T.J. would never, ever want to share it with me!

Chapter 8
Gardens Galore

Great news! The newspaper made enough money from the T-shirt sale for Granny and the Garden Club to plant gardens all around town.

Everyone has an idea for where the gardens should go. “The area by the old train station could use some sprucing up,” T.J. suggests.

“How about a garden in front of the courthouse?” Momma says. “That’d make the town square look just perfect.”

I bet you already know what kind of garden I suggested — yup, a pink garden! And Granny loved my idea!

On Tuesday, Granny and the rest of the Garden Club head over to the railroad station to plant a butterfly garden. They plant all sorts of flowers to attract the butterflies — purple coneflower, Mexican sunflower, butterfly weed, mist flowers, and butterfly bush.

Next they fill in the borders with all sorts of plants that butterflies just love like sweet peas, sunflowers, marigolds, snapdragons, and hollyhocks. Finally they set a birdbath right in the center of the garden so that the butterflies will have someplace to rest when they're tired from flying!

On Wednesday, it's time to tackle my garden! Granny loved my plan for a pretty pink garden. We found the perfect spot, too! We're planting it right in front of the public library. It's the perfect spot for me since I love to read so much!

Ugly Brother and I get to help, and I invite my friends, too. Granny is waiting for us at the library after school. The sidewalk is covered with long boxes full of flowers, and the rest of the Garden Club ladies are standing nearby.

Before long, I see Lucy. She is holding a watering can that is shaped like a sunflower.

"You look like a real true Garden Club lady with that!" I tell Lucy.

"Nanny gave it to me," she says. "Did you see Miss Clarabelle's straw hat? She looks like she is wearing a little garden on her head."

Lucy and I giggle and pull on our gloves. Ugly Brother barks and runs in a circle around us.

"Are you ready to help too?" I ask him.

He barks, "Ruff." That means no. Suddenly he runs off and starts digging through Granny's gardening bag. When he runs back, he has a pair of gardening gloves hanging from his mouth.

"Are these gloves for you, Ugly Brother?" I ask.

He barks, "Ruff, ruff."

"Oh, no!" Lucy says. "Dogs can't wear gloves. What are we going to tell him?"

I put on my thinking cap. There just has to be a way! It will break Ugly Brother's poor little heart if he can't have gloves, too. He always wants to be like everyone else.

Just then an idea hits me. I reach down and tuck the gloves into his collar. "Is that good?" I ask.

"Ruff, ruff!" he barks happily.

Cara and Paula ride up on their bikes just in time to start digging. The garden pops with hot-pink daisies, soft-pink roses, and bubble-gum-pink geraniums. The geraniums remind Paula that she has bubble gum in her pocket.

"Who wants a piece?" she asks, pulling the pink pack out of her pocket. "We can have a bubble-blowing contest while we work!"

I think that is a great idea! We all take a piece and get to work. First we dig a hole, then we blow a bubble.

Cara blows a giant bubble the size of a baseball. "I bet no one can blow a bubble bigger than that!" she says.

Paula doesn't like to lose. "I bet I can!" she says.

We all watch as Paula blows a big bubble. She blows more and more, and the bubble gets bigger and bigger. It gets so big I am worried it's going to pop.

"Be careful —" I start to say. But my warning comes too late.

There is a loud *POP!* as Paula's bubble breaks and sticks all over her face. There are blobs of pink gum in her hair, too!

Granny has to call Paula's momma to come pick her up. "I don't envy her momma," Granny says. "Getting that gum off is going to be a challenge."

"I guess I win the contest," Cara brags.

Paula starts to cry.

"Wait just a minute," I say. "Paula did blow the biggest bubble."

"Kylie Jean has a point," Lucy agrees.

We declare Paula the bubble-blowing winner right as her momma pulls up. I give her a big squeezy hug, but I'm careful not to get any of that sticky gum on me.

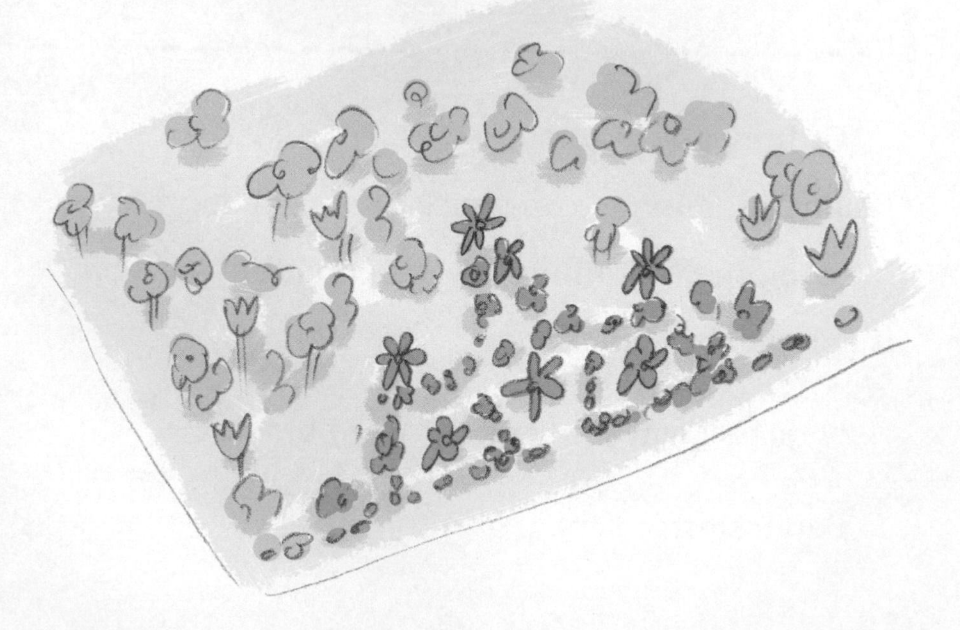

I look back at the garden and realize we are almost done. “The border of pink flowers looks almost like a crown!” I tell Granny.

“You think everything looks like a crown,” Cara says. Since my dream is to be a beauty queen, she’s right!

“We better hurry and clean up,” Granny says. “It’s getting close to suppertime.”

We clean up our supplies, and as Ugly Brother and I get ready to head home, I just have to take one more look at my beautiful pink patch of pretty flowers. It is a garden fit for a queen!

Thursday’s garden is a water garden in the middle of the town park. It has lots of lotus flowers, cattails, and lily pads. There are even fish swimming in it!

On Friday, it's time for Granny's garden — the final one. Granny decides to plant her garden in front of the town hall.

She decides to work all by herself, and at the end of the day, everyone is amazed at her magnificent garden! Granny sure did save the best for last!

In the center, plants and flowers form a giant dogwood tree. All around the edges of the garden, flowers in every color of the rainbow form a border. Butterflies flit happily over the blossoms, and bees buzz in appreciation.

At the end of the week, our little town has gardens galore! We're sure to win the Prettiest Town contest now!

TOWN HALL

Chapter 9
VIPs

It's less than a week before Earth Day, and some VIPs have come to Jacksonville! VIPs are Very Important People. Can you guess who they are? The judges for the Prettiest Town contest!

When Momma calls me downstairs for breakfast, I am all ready to go to school! I have on my Green Team T-shirt, and my hair is in a ponytail that I fixed all by myself. I check it in the mirror and see that it looks a little crooked.

"Does my hair look okay?" I ask Ugly Brother.

He barks, "Ruff, Ruff!" That means yes!

"We better get downstairs," I tell him. "I think I smell banana nut muffins for breakfast!"

In our big, sunny kitchen, breakfast is waiting on the table. I was right — there is a big plate of muffins right smack-dab in the center. Yum-O! There are glasses of milk and a pitcher of freshly squeezed orange juice, too. Daddy loves fresh OJ.

Momma gives me a kiss. "Good morning, Sweet Pea. I see Ugly Brother. Is T.J. up, too?"

"Yes, ma'am," I say with a nod.

"Your ponytail is a little crooked," Momma says. "Come over here, and let me fix it for you."

After Momma fixes my hair, Daddy comes in looking handsome in his navy suit. Momma fixes him a plate. He gives her a kiss on the cheek and opens the morning paper.

"I heard those judges stayed at the Magnolia Hotel downtown last night," Momma tells us. "I sure hope they liked it. It's the best hotel we have, and we want them to like our little town!"

"I sure hope they get to see all the important things we've been doing around town," I tell Momma. "Especially all of the beautiful gardens and trees. Do you think they will come to your newspaper, Daddy?"

Daddy shrugs. "Maybe. I'm not sure," he tells me.

Just then, I hear the bus turning the corner at the end of Peachtree Lane. I start to shout for T.J. to hurry up, but right at that very moment he dashes in, grabs two muffins, and runs to the front door. I'm right behind him.

On the bus, I sit in my best seat behind Mr. Jim. I want to talk to him about the VIPs. "Have you seen the judges for the contest?" I ask.

"I sure did!" he says. "It's two men and a young lady. She kind of reminds me of a famous actress. I can't think of her name — the one who is trying to clean up the rivers."

"What about the men?" I ask.

Mr. Jim says, "Just two fellas in suits."

I sigh. "I sure do wish I could see them," I say.

"I wouldn't get your heart set on it," he says.

Mr. Jim is probably right. I'll be in school today while they're deciding if we've won or not. I don't know it then, but I am in for one big surprise!

After lunch, Ms. Corazón is teaching our science lesson when we hear voices in the hall. The door opens, and our principal steps in with four guests. One of the men is Mayor Jenkins. The rest of the folks must be the judges. This is so exciting!

The principal says, "Ms. Corazón, our mayor told these fine contest judges all about our playground makeover. I think the students who planned the project should show it to them."

He means us! Cara, Paula, Lucy, and I go meet the judges and take them outside. I hang back and walk with the mayor. I am feeling a little anxious. "Do you think we're going to win?" I ask quietly.

"No telling," Mayor Jenkins says. "They keep making lots of notes on those clipboards they're carrying. The woman is that famous actress, Savannah Fairchild. She asks all of the environmental questions."

I see the woman talking to Lucy. I bet she wants to know about our recycling cans. Moving closer, I listen as Lucy tells her all about the student council's Recycling Roundup. Maybe if I stand beside her she'll ask me a question, too.

Ms. Fairchild turns to me. "What gave you the idea to clean up your playground?" she asks.

"I wanted to do something to celebrate Earth Day and prove that little kids can make a difference, too," I say. "But I didn't have the idea to fix up the playground. That was Cara."

"I thought it was a class project," she says.

"It was," I say. "Cara had the idea, we helped her think of a plan, and our whole class and the town came out to do the work."

Ms. Fairchild smiles. "I see. Teamwork."

Pointing to my T-shirt, I say, "Yes, ma'am. Green Team work!"

"What other things do you think kids can do to help the planet?" Ms. Fairchild asks me.

"That's easy," I tell her. "Our teacher, Ms. Corazón, taught us all about the Top Ten!"

Top Ten Ways for Kids to Save Planet Earth

1. Plant a tree or plant a garden.
2. Walk, bike, or carpool to save fuel.
3. Save water by taking shorter showers and turning off the water when you brush your teeth.
4. Power down! Turn off lights, TV, and technology to save energy.
5. Use the 3Rs: Reduce, Reuse, and Recycle.
6. Compost your fruit and vegetable scraps.
7. Trade toys, clothes, and books rather than throwing them away.
8. Speak up! Remind your parents to use cloth grocery bags and buy eco-friendly products.
9. Use recycled paper or go paperless.
10. Help raise money or awareness to save endangered animals.

Ms. Fairchild writes and writes on her clipboard. "You girls are real green leaders in your community," she tells us.

Later that night at dinner, after I share my exciting news about our special school visitors, Daddy tells us they visited his newspaper, too. "They wanted to see the brochures we've been passing out and get copies of the stories we did on green living," he says.

"I wonder where else they went," Momma says.

"Mayor Jenkins told me they visited gardens, parks, schools, recycling centers, and businesses," Daddy tells us.

"I sure hope Jacksonville made a good impression!" Momma says.

I feel good about our chances, but I say, "We are already winners! Just look at all of the good things we've been doing for our VIP — very important planet!"

Chapter 10

Parade Preparations

Jacksonville is on its way to being crowned the Prettiest Town in Texas, but there is still lots of work to be done for the Earth Day parade! For starters, we have to build the parade floats.

Daddy's newspaper is using recycled newspapers to create a little house on their float. The newspaper-delivery boy with the best delivery record gets to ride on the float and throw papers to people watching the parade.

The café is using recycled cans to make their "Eat Green" float. They borrowed a huge watering trough to use as a giant bowl and are using the cans to make pieces of fruit and veggies to put in it. I saw the string beans, and they are as tall as I am!

But hands down, the best parade float is going to be Granny's Garden Club float. They have to wait until the last minute to work on it because they are using real flowers!

Tonight we will all help with Daddy's float.

After we finish eating dinner, Daddy asks, "Ready to roll?"

"Yup!" I say.

"Let's do it!" T.J. agrees.

Momma gives Daddy a thumbs-up as she locks the door. We all head for Momma's van. We have to drive instead of walking since we will be coming home after dark.

When we get to the newspaper office, there is platform waiting for us. It is tiny compared to last year's floats, but this year everyone agreed to save energy by making their floats smaller. They'll be pulled by a four-wheeler instead of a pickup truck.

"First we'll make a frame for the little house out of chicken wire," Daddy tells us.

"I can help with that," T.J. offers.

They start building, and Momma says, "While they do that, let's lay out the recycled newspapers."

Suddenly an idea hits my brain like moss on a tree. "Let's use the plain papers for the walls and the colorful ads for the roof, door, and windows!" I suggest.

Momma smiles at me proudly. "Sugar, that's a great idea! I just love it," she says.

We get right to work, and before long, Daddy is ready for us to start putting the papers on the frame. It's hard to do without getting rips in the paper. First, Daddy uses a tool that makes a hole in each corner of a stack of papers. Next we use wire to tie them very carefully onto the frame.

When the little house is covered, we head for home. Other newspaper employees will finish the floor and the sides of the float, but making the house was our job.

By the time we get home, it is way past my bedtime, so I won't be taking a shower tonight. Oh, well — at least I am doing my part and saving water!

Momma and Daddy tuck me into bed nice and snug, and I tell Ugly Brother, "One float down and one to go!"

He barks, "Ruff, ruff."

"I just thought of something," I say. "People can watch and read Daddy's float at the same time!"

Ugly Brother doesn't say anything, but I hear him snoring. He is worn out, and he didn't even come help us tonight! I must be worn out, too, because I go right to sleep.

On Thursday night, Momma and I go over to Granny and Pappy's house to work on the Garden Club float. They are making it in the garage.

Pappy already has the frame ready. It looks like a giant dogwood tree, and all around it will be baskets of real flowers.

Everywhere I look, I see tall buckets full of fresh flowers in every hue and color. It looks like we are in the Bizzy Bee Flower Shop, and it smells like perfume!

As soon as she spots us, Granny waves. "Am I ever glad to see you two," she says. "We need all the help we can get!"

"Just put us to work," Momma says. "We came to help!"

The floor of the garage is covered with giant plastic tarps. Some of the Garden Club ladies are sitting on stools, clipping the stems of the flowers and placing them on the tarps. Momma and I get to put the flowers through the wire frame.

"I sure hope this is easier than making the newspaper house," I tell Momma.

Momma warns me to put on my garden gloves before we start. "The wire and prickly stems might cut your hands," she says.

Slipping on my gloves, I get busy pulling the flowers through the tree design. In no time at all, I have half of the tree finished. Wow! I sure am proud of myself.

Granny says, “I think your tiny hands make that the perfect job for you, Kylie Jean.”

The Garden Club ladies chat while they work. They talk way more than Daddy and T.J. do! I like to listen to them.

We haven't even been here an hour, and I already know who has a new baby, who brought the best recipes to the church potluck last night, and which salon does the best job for French tip fingernails. Now if I only knew what French tips were!

Granny is a great Garden Club president. She keeps all the ladies on track. "Y'all are doing an awesome job!" she tells everyone. "Keep it up. Just give me thirty more minutes, and we'll quit for the night. I have chocolate icebox cake and sweet tea so we can have a little snack before you head home."

Momma looks in my direction. I just know she's going to say we'll have to go soon, but that chocolate cake sure does sound tasty.

Before Momma can say it's time to leave, I beg, "Please, can we stay and have some cake? I promise to go right to sleep when we get home!"

I know I have a secret weapon in my favor. Momma's weakness is chocolate! She seems unsure, but finally makes up her mind. "Okay, but no sweet tea for you. Only milk," she tells me.

I smile real wide. "You're the best momma in the whole wide world," I tell her.

Before long everyone is in Granny's big kitchen enjoying a well-deserved treat after all our hard work. Then it's home and right to bed for me! I need my rest — Earth Day is almost here!

Chapter 11
Garden Club Queen

On Friday, I notice that something strange is going on. The contest judges are still here! They have been here all week long.

Tomorrow is Saturday, and the Garden Club is having their Earth Day luncheon. I am keeping my fingers crossed that Granny finally gets to be Garden Club president!

Mysterious things keep happening. That night while we are all watching TV, Momma gets a phone call.

When she hangs up, she tells us, "Granny says our family has been invited to the luncheon."

"Really?" I ask. I have never been to a luncheon before!

"Usually only Garden Club members attend," Momma says. "What do you think is going on?"

"I think this is a very good sign!" Daddy says. "Before you know it, I'll be calling my momma 'Madame President.'"

"Be careful, or you might jinx her," T.J. warns.

T.J. only thinks that because he's a football player. They're really superstitious. He has a pair of lucky socks that he wears for every game. They are old and stinky but so full of luck that T.J. won't let Momma throw them out.

Just then an idea hits my brain like salt on a fresh garden tomato! "T.J., you should let Granny wear your lucky socks tomorrow for the Garden Club luncheon," I say. "She'll be president for sure!"

T.J. shakes his head. "No way!" he says. "Those socks only make me lucky."

Momma doesn't agree. "Just smelling them is unlucky, so let's agree to leave them behind," she says.

The next day, we get all dressed up in our fancy church clothes to attend the Garden Club luncheon. It's being held in the Magnolia Hotel's Grand Ballroom. Momma and I wear pretty dresses with flowers on them. Mine's pink, of course. We also have on gloves and hats.

All the tables are set with fancy crystal, china, and silver and have dazzling flower arrangements in the middle. When we arrive, a waiter walks us over to a special table right in the front. There is a little sign on our table that says *RESERVED*.

"What does that mean?" I ask.

"It means they have been saving the table just for us!" Momma tells me.

Just then, I recognize someone walking toward us. “Here comes Granny!” I announce.

Daddy and T.J. stand up like real true gentlemen. T.J. pulls out Granny’s chair for her, and Daddy kisses her cheek.

“I’m as nervous as a cat in a canoe!” Granny says. “I wish they’d just serve lunch already.”

Granny has to wait for a special announcement before she gets her wish. The mayor’s wife and current Garden Club president, Lottie Jenkins, walks up to the podium to welcome everyone. She is a teeny-tiny woman wearing a humongous hat that is completely covered with silk roses.

Mrs. Jenkins says, “Mrs. Carter, would you mind joining me on stage for a moment?”

Granny makes her way up to the podium and Momma whispers, "This is it! Granny is going to be the winner!"

Mrs. Jenkins smiles and says, "Everyone, please give Mrs. Carter a round of applause for all her hard work. Thanks to her, Jacksonville has lots of new gardens for everyone to enjoy!"

Everyone claps for Granny, and I smile proudly. Granny's gardens are sure to help us win the Prettiest Town contest!

"Mrs. Carter is my dear friend and a fabulous gardener," Mrs. Jenkins continues. "And now she is also our new Garden Club president!"

People are standing, clapping, and cheering. Mrs. Jenkins hugs Granny and steps to the side. Granny says the blessing and invites everyone to enjoy a delicious lunch. Back at the table, Momma gives Granny a kiss.

“I am so proud of you!” Daddy tells her.

The waiter comes around and sets plates down in front of everyone. I think it’s supposed to be a salad, but I see flowers in with the spinach leaves.

“This is too pretty to eat!” I exclaim.

“They really do taste good,” Granny reassures me.

I'm really glad Granny is the Garden Club president, but I think Garden Club Queen sounds better. Even so, I tell her, "Granny, you know everything about gardens, and that is why you are a real true Garden Club president."

"Thank you, sugar," Granny says. "That's real nice of you."

After we eat our second course of chicken and some delicious strawberry shortcake for dessert, Granny gets up to thank everyone for coming. Mrs. Jenkins goes to the podium, too, and Granny looks confused.

In fact, everyone except Mrs. Jenkins looks confused. Suddenly the doors to the ballroom open. The mayor and the judges from the Prettiest Town contest walk in!

Mrs. Jenkins asks, "Madame President, may I please introduce some special guests?"

"Yes, please do," Granny says.

The mayor and the judges come to the front of the ballroom, and Ms. Fairchild steps up to the microphone.

"Jacksonville is a remarkable town with a great green spirit," Ms. Fairchild says. "You have lovely gardens and trees. You are pretty inside and out, and we are very pleased to name you the Prettiest Town in Texas!"

Everyone goes crazy! One of the male judges hands the mayor a giant check. It is so big that it takes two people just to hold it!

"How do you spend a check that big?" I ask.

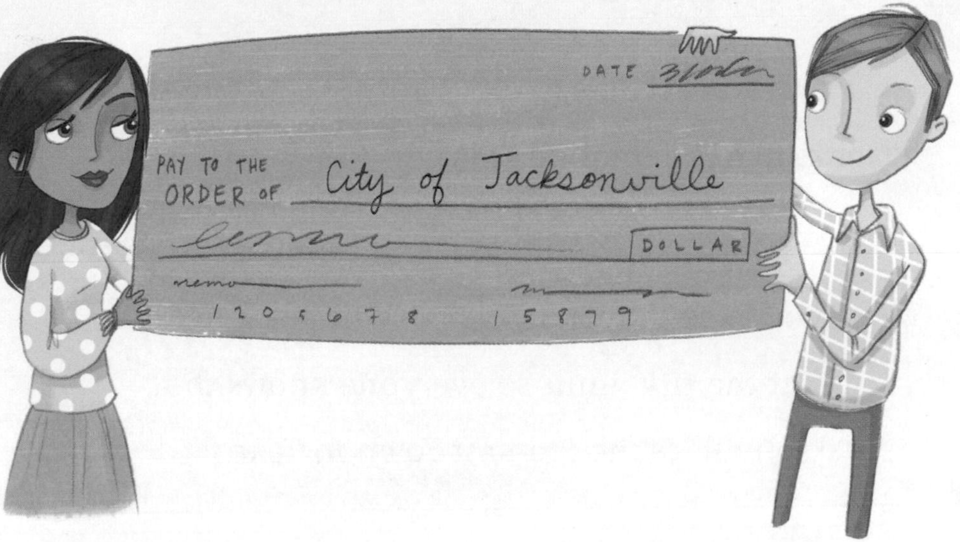

Daddy laughs and tells me, “The real check is smaller.”

The mayor steps up to the microphone next. Everyone stops cheering so he can speak.

“Jacksonville is pleased to have received such a special honor,” Mayor Jenkins says, “but it would not be possible without the vision of one fine citizen. Let’s all give Mrs. Carter another round of applause for all of her hard work!”

Everyone cheers again. Granny is so happy she looks like she might cry.

“I know just what to do with some of this prize money,” the mayor says. “We will put a new sign at the city limits so everyone knows that Jacksonville is the Prettiest Town in Texas!”

Chapter 12
Earth Day

It is finally Earth Day! My whole family wakes up bright and early to get our floats lined up for the parade.

We are all so excited to be celebrating. I put on a pretty T-shirt with pink flowers on it. Ugly Brother gets to come too. He is so excited that he keeps on waggin' his itty-bitty tail.

Momma is really worried because it looks dark and overcast outside. Black clouds hang low in the morning sky.

The weatherman on the local news is predicting rain. “If it rains, they’ll have to cancel the parade,” Momma says.

“Don’t worry,” Daddy says. “That weatherman is wrong just as much as he’s right.”

I think about the newspaper house on Daddy’s float. Wet paper is heavy. Rain will ruin everything!

But Daddy isn’t worried. He tells us, “Either we can worry, or we can get ready for the best Earth Day parade ever. Think positive. I bet the sun comes out.”

T.J. nods. “If we’re going to have a float in the parade, we’ve got to get going to get in the lineup,” he says.

Momma, Ugly Brother, and I walk down to the town square. It is already busy when we get there. There is a snow-cone stand, a face-painting station, and a band playing music. Ms. Corazón has our class's recycled art projects displayed on tables.

In the middle of the town square, right in front of the courthouse, a stage with four microphones has been set up.

On the other side of the square, the Jacksonville Recycling Center is passing out information on recycling, and the Jacksonville Library has a book-exchange table set up. Ms. Patrick, the librarian, keeps looking nervously at the cloudy sky.

"Don't worry," I tell her. "My daddy says the sun's going to come out."

"I thought your daddy was a newspaper man, not a weatherman," she says. "But either way, I sure hope he's right."

People are starting to fill up the square. I decide to get a snow cone before it's too busy. They have berry berry, mint leaf, and sunny citrus. The thing about snow cones is that the color always stays on your tongue, so I decide on mint leaf. That way my tongue can match my shirt!

I don't want Ugly Brother to feel left out, so I offer him a bite. "Ugly Brother, do you want a green tongue, too?" I ask.

He barks, "Ruff, ruff." That means yes!

Ugly Brother and I are sitting on the curb sharing our snow cone when Momma sees me. She waves while she talks to Miss Clarabelle.

I sure hope Momma doesn't notice Ugly Brother's green tongue sticking out. She doesn't believe in eating after other people or dogs. Especially dogs.

Momma always says sharing germs can make you sick. I don't know if that's true, but if you ask me, sharing treats is fun!

Pretty soon Momma, T.J., and Daddy come get me, and we pick a good spot for listening to the mayor's speech. We are right in front!

Mayor Jenkins comes out first. "Welcome, everyone, to Jacksonville's Earth Day Parade!" he says. "I have a surprise for everyone — some special guests."

Three people join him on the stage, and I can't believe my eyes! It's the VIPs!

Mayor Jenkins talks about our beautiful new trees and gardens. "We are lucky to live in the Prettiest Town in Texas, but we also have a responsibility to care for our natural resources," he tells us.

We all clap and cheer. Finally the mayor says it is time for the parade. Daddy is driving the newspaper's float, so he has to go.

"Hey, Lil' Bit, want to sit on my shoulders so you can see better?" T.J. offers.

Sometimes it's great having a big brother. "Yes, please!" I say.

Ugly Brother whines and cries.

"Sorry," I tell him. "There's no more room up here."

We hear the high school marching band before we see them. Just as they come around the corner, the sun comes out, pushing the clouds away. The twirlers come next. They have green ribbons tied onto their batons.

The café float is next, and as it turns the corner on the square, a giant strawberry rolls out of the big bowl and down Second Street. Ugly Brother starts to chase after it, and Momma has to call him back.

Next up, we see Daddy's float. It looks fantastic! The paperboy is throwing papers, and the man next to us catches one.

I can hardly wait to see the Garden Club float! Finally it appears. Granny is riding right in front of the dogwood tree I made out of flowers. She is wearing a pretty pink sundress and a sash.

All our hard work has paid off. I've never seen a more beautiful float.

When she gets closer, I call out, "Granny, Granny!"

Just as the float passes, Granny looks up and I give her my best beauty queen wave, nice and slow, side to side, with a dazzling smile. It sure is good to be a Green Queen on parade day!

Marci Bales Peschke was born in Indiana, grew up in Florida, and now lives in Texas with her husband, two children, and a feisty black-and-white cat named Phoebe. She loves reading and watching movies.

When **Tuesday Mourning** was a little girl, she knew she wanted to be an artist when she grew up. Now, she is an illustrator who lives in South Pasadena, California. She especially loves illustrating books for kids and teenagers. When she isn't illustrating, Tuesday loves spending time with her husband, who is an actor, and their two sons.

Glossary

citizen (SIT-uh-zuhn)—a resident of a particular town or city

conserve (kuhn-SURV)—to save something from loss, decay, or waste

contest (KON-test)—a competition

delicate (DEL-uh-kuht)—finely made or sensitive

endangered (en-DAYN-jurd)—something that is in danger of becoming extinct

environment (en-VYE-ruhn-muhnt)—the natural world of land, sea, and air

equipment (i-KWIP-muhnt)—the tools and machines needed for a particular purpose

remarkable (ri-MAR-kuh-buhl)—worth noticing; extraordinary

renew (ri-NOO)—to replace something old with something new

reserved (ri-ZURVD)—kept for someone to use later

trough (TRAWF)—a long, narrow container from which animals can drink or eat

1. Talk about some other ways to celebrate Earth Day. What are some ways you can think of to help preserve our planet?

2. Kylie Jean's dream is to be a beauty queen. Granny's dream is to be Garden Club president. Talk about your own dream.

3. Imagine that you're watching the Earth Day parade. Talk about the other floats you might see.

Be Creative!

1. If you could plant a garden anywhere, where would it be? Write a paragraph about it. Make sure to include what you'd plant.

2. Do you think Kylie Jean's playground plan was a good one? Come up with your own plan and drawing for a green project, just like Kylie Jean and her friends did.

3. Make a list of all the things you can do to help the environment. Which of them do you already do?

This is the perfect treat for any Green Queen!
Just make sure to ask a grown-up for help.

Love, Kylie Jean

From Momma's Kitchen

FLOWER COOKIE BOUQUET

YOU NEED:

1 tube of premade cookie dough, sugar-cookie flavor

Different colors of frosting (pink, green, yellow, and white)

Wooden cookie sticks or Popsicle sticks

A flower-shaped cookie cutter

A rolling pin

A cookie sheet

A grown-up helper

A round piece of Styrofoam

A round vase or pot

1. Ask your grown-up to help you roll out the cookie dough into a 1/4-inch thick circle. Use your cookie cutter to cut out flower shapes.
2. Insert wooden sticks about halfway into the cookie.
3. With a grown-up's help, bake cookies as directed, watching to make sure they don't get too crispy. Cool completely.
4. Decorate each cookie with frosting.
5. Push cookies on sticks firmly into the Styrofoam and place it inside your vase or pot. Now you have a cookie bouquet as yummy as it is pretty — enjoy!

Yum, yum!

THE FUN DOESN'T STOP HERE!

Discover more at www.capstonekids.com

- Videos & Contests
- Games & Puzzles
- Friends & Favorites
- Authors & Illustrators

Find cool websites and more books like this one at www.facthound.com. Just type in the Book ID: **9781479523511** and you're ready to go!